For Gill xx
J.A.

This hardcover edition published in 2014 by Boxer Books Limited.

First published in hardcover in North America in 2007 by Hyperion Books for Children.

First published in Great Britain in 2007 by Boxer Books Limited.

www.boxerbooks.com

Boxer® is a registered trademark of Boxer Books Limited

ISBN: 978-1-907152-63-4

1 3 5 7 9 10 8 6 4 2

Printed in China

All of our papers are sourced from managed forests and renewable sources

I'm not scared!

Jonathan Allen

Boxer Books

Baby Owl decided to take
Owly for a stroll in the
moonlit woods.

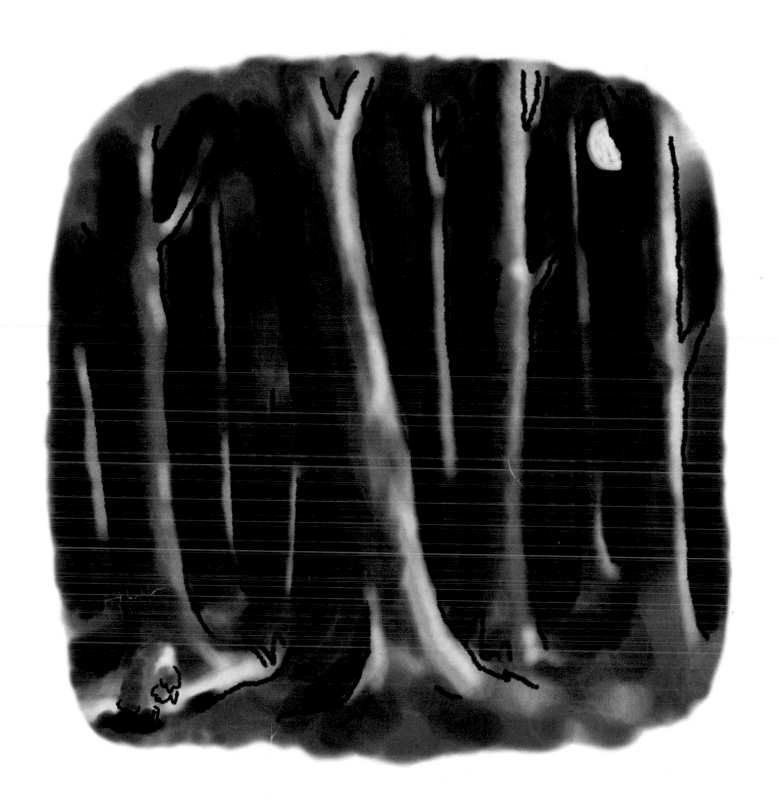

"Nobody will bother us in
the nighttime," he thought.

Then up popped Badger.
"It's only me," said Badger.
"Don't be scared, Baby Owl.

What are you doing out so late?"
she added. "It's past your bedtime."

"I'm NOT scared!" said Baby Owl.
"And it isn't past my bedtime.
I'm an owl, and owls stay up
all night!"

Then along tripped Bear.

"Oops, it's only me," said Bear.
"Don't be scared, Baby Owl."

"It's much too dark to be in the woods," he added.

"I'm NOT scared!" said Baby Owl.
"I was taking Owly for a walk, and
I can see perfectly well in the dark!"

Then down came Bat.

"It's only me," said Bat.
"Don't be scared, Baby Owl.
You shouldn't be out in the
woods at night!" she added.

"I am
NOT
scared!"
shouted Baby Owl.

"And I should be out in the woods at night. It's what owls DO!"

Then along came Dad.
"It's only me," said Dad.
"Don't be scared, Baby Owl."

"I'm NOT scared!" said Baby Owl.
"Badger, Bear, and Bat keep saying
I'm scared. But I'm not!

It's Owly who's scared!
Everyone keeps making him jump!"

"We'd better give poor Owly
a hug then," said Dad.

Baby Owl yawned a big yawn.
"The sun's coming up," said Dad.
"It's time you and Owly were
tucked up in bed."

Dad sat Baby Owl on his knee
and read him his favorite story.

Dad tucked Baby Owl into his
warm, cozy bed.
"It's okay to be a little bit scared
of the dark," whispered Dad.

"Dad means you, Owly,"
said Baby Owl.

"Goodnight, Owly."

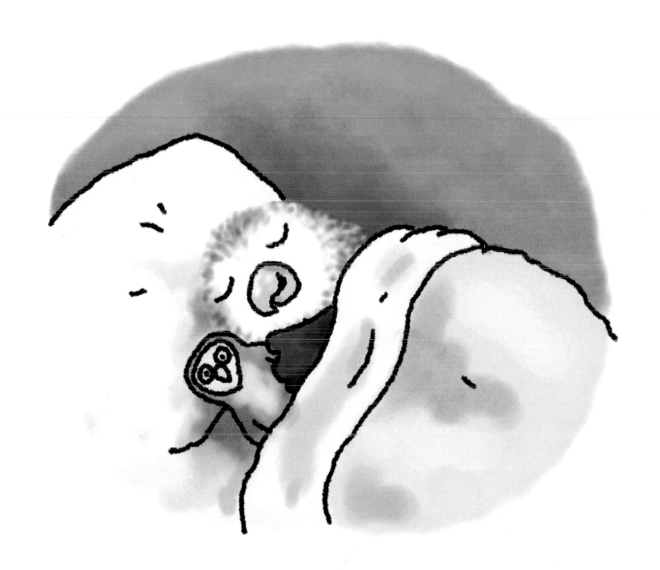